A Tail of a Different Color

by Myra Anderson

Illustrated by Debra Purchiaroni Jerome

DOT•Garnet

For Dad

Library of Congrss Cataloging-in-Publication Data

Anderson, Myra, 1953—

A tail of a different color / by Myra Anderson ; illustrated by Debra Purchiaroni Jerome.

p.   cm.

Summary: Ajax the dragon, claiming because of his golden tail to be superior to his brother Hector, mistreats him terribly, but evetually he comes to realize what is important.

ISBN 0-9625620-3-3 ; $13.95

1. Dragons–Fiction.   2. Brothers–Fiction.   3. Self-perception–Fiction.
4. Stories in rhyme.   I. Jerome, Debra Purchiaroni, ill.   II. Title
PZ8.3.A5483Tai   1992
[E]–dc20   91-29185

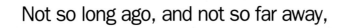

Not so long ago, and not so far away,

two dragons lived together in a cavern by the bay.

Hector was the youngest, and taller than a house,

but no matter how he tried, he was timid as a mouse.

His eyes glittered red, his scales were shiny green,

his tail shimmered purple, more royal than the queen.

His older brother, Ajax, as brave as he could be,

frightened all the rainbow crabs that lived beside the sea.

His eyes glowed misty blue and his scales were green,

but his tail shined golden, the brightest ever seen.

Their cave was filled with treasure, every size and shape

from golden-plated goblets to jewel-encrusted capes.

Rubies red as blood, and emeralds like the sea,

sapphires and diamonds, all locked up with a key.

Each morning, bright and early, they'd pack their empty sack;

down to the sea they'd travel, to bring more treasure back.

From gold doubloons to diamonds, Ajax made the choice,

while Hector did the toting, too shy to raise his voice.

All the pirates' booty that washed up from the sea

became the dragons' hunting ground from eight a.m. 'til three.

Then back up to Mt. Alvaraack and down the secret hall;

Ajax proudly led the way, while Hector carried all.

While Hector made the lemonade and fixed a tasty snack,

Brother Ajax looked at treasure, just lying on his back.

"It seems to me," said Ajax, "the time has come to choose,

divide up all the treasure, to see just whose is whose.

I think I'll take the diamonds, the silver and the gold,

and you can have the smaller gems, as much as you can hold."

"But, Ajax," spoke up Hector, "why can't we simply share?

There's plenty here for both of us, we stripped the beaches bare."

"That's true, dear brother, Hector," said Ajax with a grin.

"But there's one thing you're missing." And he lifted up his chin.

He pulled back his shoulders, he puffed up his green chest,

he buffed his long, sharp fingernails, and dusted off his vest.

"Although you may have gathered and carried more than I;

I deserve the larger share, let me tell you why.

I've thought about it long and hard, I'm sure you will agree.

Your tail is purple, mine is gold; it's clear enough to see.

Purple is so common, it's everywhere you look,

I'm sure you must have seen it in the flowers by the brook.

But gold, now that's another tale, especially it's mine,

so rare and shining, bright and glowing, positively fine.

There you have the reason for my sensible demands;

I'm simply better than you are, I'll leave it in your hands."

Hector's scales lost their glow, he shed a giant tear,

his shoulders slumped, his stomach sunk, his heart filled up with fear.

"I'm sorry that you feel this way, is all that I can say.

Except, if that's the way things are, then I must go away."

Ajax answered clearly, "Then go on, I don't need you.

I've lots of treasure by my side, I won't be feeling blue."

So Hector packed a little bag and tied it to a stick,

hung it from his shoulder and left the cavern quick.

He didn't know quite where to go or even what to do,

his heart was surely broken, his spirit turned to blue.

He finally settled on a cave, not too far from home,

near enough to smell the sea, he didn't want to roam.

He'd brought no treasure with him, he wanted none to keep.

He curled up in the corner and cried himself to sleep.

Ajax hardly missed him, he was busy as can be,

counting gold and silver, and all that he could see.

He counted every gold doubloon and every emerald ring.

Then he opened up his great big mouth and he began to sing.

He sang an ancient dragon song of treasure in the deep.

He sang until his throat was sore and then he went to sleep.

In the morning, Ajax woke and went down to the sea;

he gathered still more treasure, while humming, "all for me."

When he finally made it slowly back to Mt. Alvaraack,

he found no one was waiting, and no one made the snack.

He said, "I don't need Hector, I don't need anyone."

But counting out the treasure had lost some of its fun.

"He'll come back by nightfall…he needs me…he'll see."

And he went about his dragon things and waited patiently.

But Hector wasn't coming back, his heart was broke in two.

Why did Ajax say those things? He didn't have a clue.

So Hector changed his habits, he scoured the beach by night,

he gathered golden treasure beneath the soft moonlight.

He wasn't really happy, but his heart began to heal,

color doesn't matter, it's what's inside that's real.

Ajax wasn't sleeping well, or scouring the beach,

he wasn't counting treasure, though much was in his reach.

He'd learned a hard, hard lesson, his heart began to melt.

He knew he was no better, he knew how Hector felt.

So early one cold morning he set out on his own,

searching not for treasure, but a friend to call his own.

Sometime later that same day, about a half past three,

Ajax spotted Hector, who was heading out to sea.

"Hector," called his brother, "you were right and I was wrong."

"Ajax, you're my brother, and I've loved you all along."

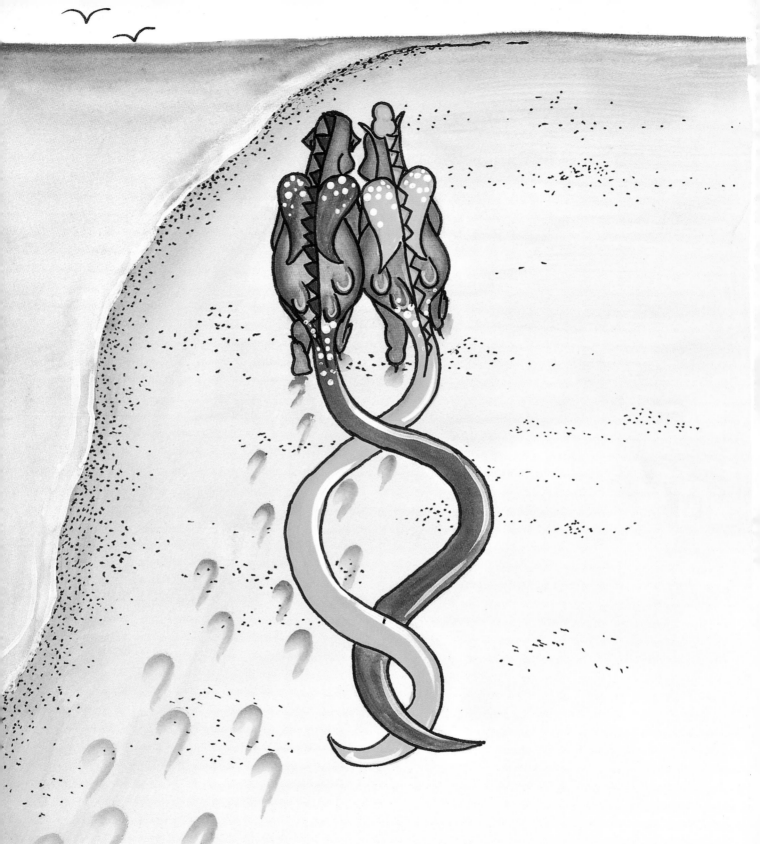

Side by side, with tails entwined, they slowly went on back,

and when they finally reached their cave…Ajax made the snack.